Something Wicked This Way Comes

Volume One

This is the first volume in a collection of ghostly tales. My intention is to release subsequent volumes with new stories in October every year to follow. I do hope that you enjoy these, but also that they do not keep you up all night, worried about what's under the bed!

Annie

Something Wicked This Way Comes

Volume One

by

Anne Katheryn Hawley

Conundrum Books and Music

conundrumbooksandmusic.com

ISBN: 978-0-9964370-1-1

Library of Congress Control Number: *Pending*

Printed in the United States of America

Conundrum:

A riddle whose answer is a pun;

A question or problem having only a conjectural answer;

An intricate or delicate problem.

"Fiction reveals truth that reality obscures."

Ralph Waldo Emerson

Death Comes to Ambrose

He was an odd duck. And not particularly good-looking either. But he was rich. Despite his great fortune, he was quite unfortunate.

Andrew Parchwood actually looked a bit like his name … parched wood. He was bony and angular, and having spent so much time on the sea and shore, his skin was weathered and dry. At only 18 years of age he had become an orphan and had inherited his parent's estate – a palatial stone and wood mansion built on their very own private island off the coast of Maine. This island was located approximately five miles off the rocky shore of Eastport, the Northeast edge of where the mighty ocean met the inhospitable and sparsely populated land.

After coming over from England, the family had made their millions in the lucrative paper mill industry.

John Parchwood and his brother, Nigel, had purchased over a thousand heavily wooded acres in northern Maine, and then opened the paper mill just east of Waterville.

The Parchwoods also bought a stately home in Boston, where the ship from England had deposited the family when they first arrived. Andrew's parents, mostly his mother, were austere, stand-offish people, and not well-liked by the locals. Their British accents and detached personalities created the superior-than-thou reputation the family was known for, but truth be told, his fragile mother, Katheryn, was almost *deathly* afraid of people. She was unreasonably shy, with possibly a bit of agoraphobia. Andrew's father, John, was simply a workaholic, and invested all of his time and energy into building his business, with Nigel at his side. Nobody knew where the family money for their purchases had originated, and nobody asked.

Ambrose was the name they had christened the huge, rambling granite and oak mansion on the island. John had purchased the lonely island and had built the monstrosity for his frail, feeble and fearful wife, Katheryn, in order to provide her with a sanctuary in which to hide away from civilization. At her request, they kept a *minimal* number of servants - only enough to clean, cook, and keep the grounds. These servants had to work double-time due to the inadequate staffing. But they were well-compensated and therefore didn't complain.
During the winter months they also hired a hearth boy, who kept the many fireplaces perpetually stocked and stoked. Otherwise they would have frozen to death.

Though Katheryn was afraid of people, she was not afraid of being alone on this rocky, isolated island, nor of the mammoth, echoing estate.

Neither was Andrew. As a child, he spent hours collecting shells and rocks from the miles of shoreline surrounding their little archipelago. With his British coloring of very pale skin and reddish, almost white-blonde hair, he was sensitive to the sunlight. He often suffered rather serious sunburns, despite the copious amounts of the thick and greasy petroleum jelly slathered onto his face by his mother.

As he became older, his father hired a tutor for Andrew. This tutor had a young daughter by the name of Mary whom he brought along to live with him there at the mansion while he provided lessons in the three R's. Andrew and Mary became fast friends.

Mary's beloved mother had died of influenza years prior. Craving maternal attention, she desperately tried to endear the affection of Andrew's mother, but Katheryn would have none of it. She remained cool and aloof, and reprimanded Andrew sharply whenever she discovered the two of them playing together.

The disapproval only served to create an even stronger bond between the two children, followed by the aphrodisiac inducing thrill of sneaking around behind Katheryn's back as the children became adolescents. The two fell in love.

Summers may have proven lonely to Andrew, as the tutoring only took place from early autumn until late spring. Mary and her father would move back to the mainland during that time. But Andrew's father, John, began to insist that Andrew was now old enough to start accompanying him to the logging camp and "learn the trade" throughout these companionless summer months. *This* Andrew did not enjoy, nor did he have one iota of interest in learning. It was a dangerous trade, as Andrew cruelly experienced at seventeen years of age. This was when Andrew witnessed the tragic death of his father. Of the very trees that had provided the family with their vast fortune, a massive oak that was being felled unexpectedly deviated from its anticipated direction as it crashed to the earth. John Parchwood was crushed only mere feet from where his bewildered son stood. This horrific event changed Andrew's life considerably. He vowed to never set foot again at the logging camp. He returned to Ambrose, where his mother, Katheryn, became even more reclusive than ever without her husband to keep her grounded.

Thus, Andrew was cut loose from the somewhat oppressive manner of parenting to which he was accustomed. He was free! And he went a little crazy with that freedom. Andrew began to make frequent trips to their Boston estate, in which Nigel had been living for many years.

Upon John's death, Nigel had been given the responsibility of making sure that Katheryn and Andrew were cared for, along with running the business. He had never really liked Katheryn, and so avoided Ambrose by simply sending provisions on a regular basis to the island. Rather than taking on a paternal role toward Andrew, he instead treated him as a comrade, and began introducing him to the numerous Boston pubs. The two became drinking buddies and often could be heard singing, and quite loudly, as they staggered through the streets in the wee hours of early morning.

Many young women, knowing full well of the ample wealth of the rather homely Andrew, would practically throw themselves at him, flirting shamelessly. As tempting as it was for Andrew, his heart had long ago been given completely to Mary.

However, his raucous behavior had been earning him a reputation - a reputation that somehow reached Mary's ears up in Portland, Maine. She expeditiously made the journey to Boston, where she and a very penitent Andrew got married. At first, they remained at the grand home in Boston, though they kept to themselves. Whenever Nigel came back from the paper mill, he and Andrew would take to the pubs – a source of great contention for the newly married couple.

So, when Katheryn died from hypothermia after banning the hearth boy from coming to tend the fire in her bedroom, Mary was only too happy to suggest that she and Andrew return to Ambrose. Upon their homecoming they found the palatial structure and grounds to be in quite a state of disrepair and dilapidation. They set about putting things back in order, with Mary taking control as the new lady of the manor. In fact, it was uncanny at how Mary began to resemble Katheryn in her demeanor and attitude. Uncanny, but maybe not so unexpected. After all, her youth had been spent primarily in this household, with Katheryn her only maternal influence and role model. Mary and Andrew made the decision to let the few servants go, as they had failed to maintain the home after Katheryn's death anyway. Mary and Andrew would simply run things on their own. They didn't mind the work, and Mary preferred the solitude, away from the maddening crowds of civilization.

Mary miraculously became pregnant!

Everything changed for the couple practically overnight. Mary somehow came back to life, and they were once again in love. The highly anticipated baby gave them a new sense of purpose and happiness, and their devotion to each other was renewed. When the blessed child arrived, Mary was overcome by her overwhelming love and affection for the tiny creature. She never slept. Instead, as the baby slept, whom they had named Katheryn in honor of Andrew's mother, Mary would vigilantly sit by the cradle, gazing lovingly at her baby girl. While Andrew shared in this utter delight for the child, he soon became acutely aware of somehow being left in the cold. Mary no longer seemed to be even aware of his presence, or to care about him at all.

Until the night that his glaring lack of presence became noticeable.

Andrew had left the island four days prior to go and collect supplies as usual. He had never before stayed on the mainland for three nights. Mary's mind once again turned to thoughts of Andrew's possible misbehavior, or her suspicion of such. She was livid. Another two long and distressing days passed with no sign or word from Andrew.

The weather had turned quite nasty, with hefty winds and bouts of heavy rain from the blackened clouds above. Mary began to get worried. *Very* worried. Not only for the missing Andrew, but also for her precious baby and herself. Supplies were running low. The wood piles needed replenishing, and Mary was *not* about to go out and chop wood! Katheryn began to cry inconsolably, sensing her mother's increasing alarm. Mary paced in the rooms, watching the vast expanse of ocean from the long span of windows, searching for any sign of Andrew's boat.

Three more days dragged by. The storms continued in a strange and scattered pattern, and the skies remained dark gray. For the first time at Ambrose, Mary got scared. She was becoming frantic. Poor little Katheryn was practically screaming insistently and incessantly. Their cavernous castle was becoming quite cold.

So Mary made a decision. She had been eyeing their little dinghy for a few days now, contemplating the journey to the mainland. The morning had shown some promise, though not much, with an occasional break in the clouds. It was as good a time as any. Mary bundled Katheryn up in blankets, and wrapping herself in one of Andrew's heavy rain coats, she made her way down the rocky slope to the dock where the dinghy was tethered. She placed Katheryn on the floor of the craft at her feet, then pulled the oars from the inside of the walls, slipping them clumsily into their oar locks.

She sat on the uncomfortable wooden bench seat, pointing the bow toward the distant shore that was not even visible at this point.

But it wasn't long before the small and insufficient boat was being pummeled in all directions by the angry waves. Mary began to panic as she realized she had no control of the vessel. Katheryn's terrified, high-pitched wail, though lost to some degree in the winds that had whipped up all around them, was acutely heard by an increasingly frenzied Mary.

A massive and unforgiving wave splashed forcefully over the side of the dinghy, and as Mary helplessly watched, Katheryn was efficiently lifted out of the worthless boat to disappear quickly into the mighty and monstrous ocean. Mary howled the most blood-curdling and heart wrenching scream.

It seemed to erupt from the depths of her very soul, and then Mary plunged off the side of the dinghy and into the furious waters after her beautiful baby girl.

Had she only given it twenty-four more hours! The very next day brought sunshine and blue skies, and with it came Andrew, so very happy and anxious to be heading back to his wife and daughter. As he glided through the now fairly tranquil waters, he barely avoided hitting the little empty dinghy, floating freely and mysteriously without a passenger.

Of course, he recognized it immediately as his own, and though a feeling of dread and fear passed through him, he surmised that the boat had somehow come loose from the dock. The one thing that seemed ominously amiss was that the oars were independently flapping around in their fixed position on the oar locks of the boat, suggesting that *someone* had perhaps moved them to be used.

No. Surely not, he thought as he nervously made his way toward his home and family.

Realization hit Andrew hard when he arrived to an empty house and island. He dropped to his knees and cried the mournful sobs of a man wrecked. He circled the small island in vain, desperately searching for his beloveds, his salty tears hot in contrast to the icy salt water of the cruel ocean tides.

His shoes ripped to shreds as he sloshed through beds of seaweed, investigating forgotten caves, and ignoring his barnacle-sliced feet, legs and hands as he climbed over rocky shoreline and implored God to return his wife and child.

He finally gave up with such a feeling of defeat and emptiness that he felt he would soon die of sorrow. He returned to the empty house and fell to the floor in the entryway, succumbing to his physical and emotional exhaustion.

Why? Why?

Andrew blamed himself, and over the next few days would not eat. In fact, the provisions were still stored away in his boat.

Then, one night as he lay on his bed in an emaciated stupor, *he heard it*!

It was a little hard to decipher exactly what the sound was at first, but it became louder, more insistent … *a baby's cry*!

Andrew did not hesitate. He ran out to the shore and began his frantic search once again. When he was completely spent, he returned to the house. He needed sustenance if he was going to have enough energy to find his family!

So he unloaded the provisions, and ate like the starved man that he was.

That night he heard the cries again. They were out there – *somewhere*! Mary and Katheryn! His nocturnal searches for them became his way of life. Andrew would eat and sleep during the day, and then the baby's doleful keening and whimpering would call to him. In vain he hoped for the impossible.

Andrew was slowly going mad.

For a time, Nigel lived in blissful ignorance of the tragedy and subsequent downward spiral of his dear nephew. But when weeks passed without seeing hide nor hair of Andrew, Nigel got to wondering how the family was getting by without their supplies – especially with a new baby to take care of.

An uneasiness crept over him, and so he decided to make the relatively short voyage over to the island to check up on things.

As he disembarked and surveyed the house and grounds, he knew something was terribly wrong. The previously groomed yard was overgrown with weeds, and the house, so solidly built by his and John's own hands, was in a sad state of neglect. The front door stood ajar, and as Nigel entered, the putrid smell of unwashed clothing and unbathed bodies, spoiled food, and general filth hit him like a brick wall. The interior was dark and dusty … and deathly quiet.

He walked through the lower level, amazed at the poor condition of the once beautiful estate, shaking his head with disbelief.

Suddenly, he heard loud footsteps quickly clamoring down the staircase. Andrew appeared before him, disheveled and somewhat deranged looking.

"Oh … it's just you, Nigel!" he said in a rushed and disappointed tone.

"Who were you expecting? And where is Mary?"

Andrew's eyes grew wide and wild as he responded,

"They're … *out there*! Somewhere out there! I've been out looking for them every night. I can hear them, but I can't find them!"

And then Andrew broke down into a sobbing, shaking heap to the floor.

It took some considerable time and patience for Nigel to coax the story out of Andrew. It came out in bits and pieces, but when it dawned on Nigel what had likely happened, he was both horrified and heartbroken for the poor, broken man.

He helped Andrew to the kitchen, where he built a fire in the woodstove after collecting some wood from outside. He poured the two of them each a large snifter of brandy, and then rummaged around in the cupboards until he found some potatoes, onions and a bowl of pork fat.

Nigel fried it up on the stove and placed the steaming plate in front of Andrew. It was the first hot meal that Andrew had eaten in weeks, and he devoured it like a man famished.

Nigel *had* to bring Andrew back to reality, but was unsure as to the fragility of his mind. These midnight searches needed to stop before they killed the young man. Winter would soon be here, and besides that, he needed to get Andrew off this island and away from this house.

"Andrew," he began authoritatively.

Andrew looked up expectantly from his plate.

Sometimes you had to be cruel to be kind, so Nigel said "You do know they're *gone*, don't you?"

"NO! No … *they are out there*! My little Katheryn cries out to me every evening! I hear it quite clearly! If I could only *find* them!" he bellowed deliriously.

There would be no talking sense to this man. Nigel was going to have to trick him off the island somehow, and then get him into a lunatic asylum for help. So instead of fighting a losing battle with the pitiful, deluded man, he played along with the insanity.

"Well then, Andrew, maybe we should get a search party from the mainland to help us. Let's talk about it in the morning, but for now, we should both get a good night's sleep."

Andrew nodded solemnly as he contemplated this. The warm food was bringing a sense of calm and sleepiness to him, and his red-rimmed eyes were already at half-mast.

So Nigel assisted the reed-thin man up the stairs, finding clean blankets to cover him up in the chilly house. He went back outside to collect more wood in order to build a fire in the bedroom, and then lit some of the kerosene lanterns that had any remaining fuel in them. When he returned, Andrew was fast asleep.

Nigel then went back down to the kitchen to sit by the woodstove and mull over the situation.

He had *promised* his brother should anything ever happen to him that he would look after Andrew, and *just look at what had happened* under his failed guidance. His guilt and sense of responsibility for this devastation were overwhelming.

He cried as he prayed for his brother John's forgiveness, until he finally dozed off.

The fire in the stove had burned out, as had the kerosene lantern on the table. The night was black when Nigel awoke with a start. The glow of a high moon cut a diagonal slash of light across the wooden floor. It was strangely quiet until he heard the sharp bang of the front door flapping in the gusts, followed by the very distinguishable cry of a baby being carried on the wind.

His heart began to pound and his mouth got dry as the crying got louder and louder from outside.

He quickly ran up the stairs to check on Andrew, and found the covers thrown to the floor and no Andrew in sight. He immediately went over to the window to look out at the shore in front of the house.

The shock of what he saw made him recoil in horror.

The image of Mary, though transparent and misty, was very recognizable. She was coming up out of the ocean waters, a ghostly baby in one arm. Her other arm was outstretched as though beckoning. The baby was still crying, but Mary was laughing. A low, barely audible laughter.

Nigel was frozen in place until he saw Andrew running toward the apparition.

He began to pound violently on the thick, wavy glass of the window, shouting Andrew's name at the top of his lungs, but Andrew was oblivious to it. Instead, his focus was fixed upon his beloved family as he pushed through the waves to join them.

Nigel powerlessly watched as the ghost of Mary took Andrew by the hand, and she, the baby, and his nephew disappeared below the surface of the churning, frothy sea, never to be seen again - alive.

The island remains deserted to this day, the old mansion crumbling to ruins. The ghosts of Andrew, Mary and Katheryn have been sighted by brave souls who have dared venture there, but these haunting spirits prevent anyone from settling there again. And that's just how Mary likes it.

The Twins in the Window

You could still smell the smoke and ashes. Stepping foot inside the burned out shell of a building was strictly forbidden. *Had our parents only known!*

In its heyday, the structure had been quite a grand and stately mansion, but now it was a sad and forlorn remnant of sooty ruins. Neighborhood delinquents were known to play games like "doctor" or "spin the bottle" in that dilapidated danger zone. Someone should have boarded the thing up.

Oh wait, they *did*, not that it made any difference to us.

We always found a way to get inside. It was perpetually as cold as a November night in that old house. Even in the middle of August during a heat wave! And it was kinda spooky too, which is why nobody ever went there after dusk. Even in broad daylight I remember the hair standing up on the back of my neck suddenly, and without discernible reason, on more than one occasion.

“Your turn,” urged Esther as she pushed the empty coca-cola bottle over to Russell. He and Jacob were our token boys. We had an unfair ratio of two-boys-to-four-girls. That meant that Russell and Jacob took turns kissing whichever of us ridiculous, skinny, bandaid-kneed girls the bottle happened to point toward: me, Esther, Maureen or Abbey.

This time, the lucky girl was me. The thrill of it was mixed with an awkward self-consciousness and apprehension that never failed to make my palms sweat profusely and give me the uncontrollable urge to giggle.

We all giggled, for ourselves and for each other – the coming-of-age experimenting-with-love type of giggle.

For privacy while the clandestine kissing took place, the two “kissees” were to walk over behind a half-wall which was scorched black, but with patches of bubbled-up, burned wallpaper on which a tiny rose print was still distinguishable, but barely recognizable.

Russell and I dropped to our dirty, boney knees, facing each other with goofy grins plastered to our faces.

Mine was especially goofy, as I desperately needed braces, which my parents couldn’t afford.

My buck teeth did not seem to hinder Russell. He reached out with both hands to grasp my shoulders in a death grip that was evidence of his own anxiety, and pulled me toward his face. Our tightened, puckered lips met in what was more of a *collision* than a kiss. *What did we know?*

But then Russell loosened his vise-like grip on my shoulders, this time pulling me in more gently, and with purpose.

My twelve-year old inexperience was about to be tested, but the moment was abruptly interrupted by the chilling screams that pierced the room. This was one of those times when the hair on the back of my neck stood up – this time like a million tiny ice-picks that spread like dominoes down my spine. Russell and I scrambled to our feet and joined the others in the mad dash we made to high-tail it out of there.

The fear in the air was contagious, and I caught a bad case of it. We were all screaming at that point, taking turns climbing out the window with the loosened boards that we had entered through. Russell was the last to exit.

"*What just happened*?" demanded Esther breathlessly when we reached a safe distance from the house.

"Didn't you SEE?" asked Maureen with horrified incredulity.

"I didn't see anything, but I *felt* it!" returned Esther, eyes big as Frisbees. "It was like someone opened a freezer door!"

"They walked right through us!" exclaimed Jacob.

"Who's *they*?" asked Russell.

"They were *kids*! *Dead kids*!"

"I saw'em!"

"I saw'em too!"

Although Russell, Esther and I did not actually see the apparitions that our three friends claimed to have witnessed, we had no doubt that the claim was true.

There had been a feeling of terrible dread, an ominous force that had permeated the air. I felt it overtake my entire being just prior to the onslaught of piercing screams, one of which was my own.

In that split second I had attributed it to the inevitable "real kiss" that I had been about to receive.

But now I knew without doubt that an entity, *two* actually, from beyond the grave had been the cause.

Of course, this "event" had been the talk of the neighborhood for weeks to follow.

As parents found out what their kids had been up to, there was the piper to pay. Some of us were "grounded", while others of us, like me, got a good whooping. The adults then took it upon themselves to hire a professional to securely board up any of the accessible windows and doors of the old house. It became an impenetrable fortress.

Eventually the rumors and tales of the *dead kids* faded into the background of new rumors and stories, most of which had to do with who was "in love" with whom at any given moment. Adolescence kicked into gear and our focus shifted.

I went away to attend college at The University of Maine in Orono, where I met the man who would become my husband, John Brown. My parents were thrilled with my choice, as he was as devout a Catholic as I had been raised to be.

So on one beautiful, balmy autumn weekend, I brought John home with me for a visit and the gluttonous Sunday afternoon dinner that my mom was so famous for. John and I decided to go to the Sunday afternoon mass so we could sleep in (in separate bedrooms of course!).

As we strolled arm in arm toward the church, we happened to pass by the old, still burned out and boarded up haunted estate.

I hadn't even given the place a smidgeon of thought in years, and that day was no exception. My thoughts instead were dreaming of the wedding that would take place in the church we were now headed toward.

But suddenly John stopped short. Just as abruptly, those same icy needles from so many years before jumped to a sharp attention along the back of my neck, quickly spreading both upward over my scalp and downward along my spine. I followed his terrified gaze to an upper story window, where the ghostly images of two young boys stared blankly at us before dissipating into nothingness.

"Did you just see what I saw?" he asked in a high-pitched, tight whisper.

I just stood there, my mouth hanging open in shock and disbelief. There was a sense of agonized sorrow and distress in the air – that is the only way I can explain it. We were temporarily immersed in this feeling, along with an immediate cold chill.

John and I just looked at each other, at a loss for words. He quickly pulled on my arm and we resumed our walk to church, but at a brisk pace.

When we reached the safety of hallowed ground, we decided to sit on a bench to talk about what we had just seen.

The memory of the spin-the-bottle episode was acutely clear, like it had just happened yesterday. I told John the tale. By the tone of my voice and the look of real fear on my face, he knew I was telling a true story. We then entered the church to pray for our salvation and the Lord's protection from all things evil.

We took the long way home, far from that eerie edifice.

When we arrived back at my parent's house, they were in the living room watching television. They could see right away by the looks on our faces that something was very wrong.

Now, my parents had heard the story of the ghostly kids interrupting our "kid's meeting" (which is the lie part of what we told the adults at the time).

They never knew what we were *really* up to that day, as nobody would admit the "spin-the-bottle" part. They very likely suspected though.

So as John and I sat down in the armchairs facing the couch on which my parents were

sitting, now at rapt and anticipatory attention, and after turning the television off, I began by reminding them of that story from my past, unsure if they would even remember.

Oh, they remembered alright.

I then turned it over to John, who recounted what we had just experienced. He tried to sound very matter-of-fact as he spoke, almost scientific, like there *must* have been some plausible explanation. But you could clearly hear the tremulous angst in his voice.

Watching my parents' faces turn a whiter shade of pale only served to bring the terror to the surface as I too, listened to John's telling.

My father then stood wearily, as he looked hesitantly and questioningly at my mother, who only nodded at him.

"Wait here." he said.

Mom, John and I sat in silence until my father's return to the room. When he reappeared, he was holding an old newspaper in his hands. It was dated October 13th, 1956. It was yellowed and brittle – not surprising for a paper almost 25 years old.

Dad delicately delivered it into John's hands, and I peered over John's shoulder as we read the headlines together:

PROMINENT ATTORNEY CONFESSES TO MURDERING YOUNG WIFE AND SETTING FIRE TO HOUSE WHERE TWIN SONS PERISH IN BLAZE.

We continued to read with a mixture of dread, disbelief and complete horror.

The article described the husband as a wealthy tax attorney by the name of Leopold Pelletier, who had married a much younger and stunningly beautiful woman, Deloris McKenna. The twin sons were hers from a previous relationship. She had never married their father. Leopold had spared no expense when he had the gorgeous Victorian house built for his new bride and step-sons. For all outward appearances, they seemed to be a content family and happy couple.

Later, as witnesses to the relationship attested, Leopold had actually been a jealous and controlling man, who had kept close tabs on his lovely wife. It was also later revealed that Deloris had secretly been stealing away to maintain a relationship with her sons' father. Leopold had apparently found out. He slit his bride's throat after following her to her lover's flat, and then, left her to bleed out on the side of the road. He returned to his mansion, and as the five year old boys slept soundly in their second floor bedroom, he spread kerosene throughout the house, setting it afire.

Their charred bones were recovered after the raging inferno was extinguished.

After confessing to the crimes, Leopold hung himself in his jail cell, using his bed sheets as a noose.

The Red-haired Girl

Although this tale includes an excerpt from my fictional novel, *Careful What You Wish For*, it is based on a true experience, one that inspired that story – and one that has led me to have an unwavering belief in angels. Here is the *untold* part of that story!

She couldn't swim. At only six years of age, she felt ashamed and embarrassed about this shortcoming.

Especially now.

Meggie had been invited to spend the day at China Lake! Kimmy Buckley, who spent the summers with her grandmother, was a year older than Meggie, but the two played together often; that is, when her grandmother allowed it. She only lived the next street over, but seemed to think that Meggie and her mother were from "the other side of the tracks". At least she acted that way, according to Meggie's mom.

Meggie was more than thrilled to be graced with the invitation.

Opportunities like this didn't present themselves to her all that often, and so far, this had been one incredibly hot, muggy, and unbearable August. But today she was going to the lake!

Meggie's mom had the breakfast shift at Denny's, so Meggie dug her bathing suit out of the pile of clothing on the closet floor, scoffed down a bowl of cheerios, grabbed a towel from the bathroom, and ran over to Kimmy's grandmother's house.

She was worried that they would leave without her—that they hadn't really meant it or something—which is why she ran all the way.

But there they were, waiting patiently for her.

They piled into Kimmy's grandmother's rusty Buick, and off they went.

The first disaster of the day happened after only about 30 minutes of the hour-long drive from Bangor to Winslow.

Meggie got carsick.

Kimmy's grandmother did not even attempt to hide her disgust as she cleaned up the stomach-acid and cheerio-remnant mess at the first gas-station-slash-convenience-store they'd come to. Thank goodness they sold cleaning supplies.

"I'm sorry," Meggie whispered to the back of the headrest as Kimmy's grandmother *whumpffed* back into the driver's seat.

Kimmy hung over the passenger seat, holding her nose and giggling as she said to Meggie, "That was GROSS!"

"Turn around and sit down Kimmy! Meggie, do you think you can make it the rest of the way?" asked Kimmy's grandmother with exasperation.

The interior of the car now stunk of vomit and Mr. Clean. Kimmy's grandmother was forced to open all the windows which allowed the oppressive heat to blow into the car.

It felt more like a hairdryer than a pleasant wind, but it did help to eliminate the stench.

As they finally neared the China Lake area, the aroma of balsam fir tinged the air—a very pleasant change.

The upchuck episode was forgotten as they turned onto the wood-chipped drive, and the dark green, soft-needled branches swept fleetingly into the still open windows as they passed.

“We’re here! We’re here!” shouted Kimmy excitedly.

Kimmy’s grandmother looked into the rear-view mirror to smile at Meggie. She now felt badly for the way she had treated the poor girl for something that she couldn’t have helped.

“Meggie? Are you feeling better?” she asked.

"Yes Ma'am." Meggie had been well-trained to respect her elders.

"Do you like to swim?"

"Yes Ma'am!" Meggie was starting to anticipate jumping into the cool water, and temporarily forgot her plight about not being able to swim.

The rustic cottage at the end of the driveway they had pulled into was very secluded, but with a nice waterfront about fifty feet from the structure. It belonged to Kimmy's grandmother's bosom buddy, Ms. Toni, as she was introduced.

Ms. Toni and Kimmy's grandmother exchanged greetings in bird-chirp-like twitters, and then quickly began discussing their favorite soap opera …

"Can you believe what Nikki has done now?"

"Well, Victor pushed her to it!"

The Young and the Restless would be starting shortly, and both women were anxious to get inside so as not to miss a detail.

As they made their way into the cottage, Ms. Toni reminded Kimmy that the water toys were in the boathouse.

Kimmy's grandmother instructed them to *stay near the dock*, and then the two women disappeared to martinis and their "stories".

The sights, sounds and smells filled Meggie's senses. This was a whole other world from the one she knew. The water lapping at the pebble-strewn beach was crystal-clear.

The lake was surrounded by dense evergreen trees, which created a privacy and peacefulness that made Meggie think that *maybe* Ms. Toni owned the *entire* lake. The contrast of the vibrantly verdant trees against the brilliant azure sky, punctuated by impossibly white, fluffy clouds was so dazzling that it made Meggie's eyes water. She inhaled the heavy pine scent and somehow believed that this must be what heaven was like.

"Come on!" cried Kimmy with a degree of both excitement and impatience as she ran toward the old, weathered boathouse.

Meggie followed, her flip-flops flap-flapping against the bottoms of her feet as she, too, ran toward the shore.

She stopped at the water's edge, suddenly considering just how deep this beckoning water might be.

The water at the first foot or two of shoreline was so transparent that Meggie could see every rock at the bottom, but then it seemed to get abruptly very dark blue, which left the depth to question.

Kimmy dragged out a little blow-up boat that not only was still inflated, but did not appear to have any holes in it either.

"Let's swim first, and then take this boat out for a spin!" *Everything* Kimmy said was an exclamation.

Meggie kicked up some of the sparkling water with her feet, losing one of her flip-flops in the process.

"I'll get it!" shouted Kimmy as she ran and jumped full-barrel into the chilly water.

"AAAAAHHHH!" she screeched as she came to the surface. "It's FREEZING! Jump in, Meggie!" Kimmy laughed and splashed at Meggie.

Holding her ineffectual hands up in front of her to ward off the onslaught of the surprisingly cold water, she managed to blurt out,

"But I can't swim!"

"What do you mean, you can't swim? How old *are* you, anyway?"

"I'm six."

"Well *I* learned when I was FOUR! I learned at the pool!"

The community pool was only a block from Meggie's house. Every summer they offered swimming lessons for which they charged a dime per lesson.

After that, in order to be able to swim freely in the pool, a "tadpole test" had to be passed for which they also charged a dime.

The dime for this necessity of life had never been offered, nor had Meggie ever dared to ask for.

Being raised by a single mom who struggled to make ends meet as a waitress didn't afford luxuries like *life survival skills*. Besides, Meggie's mom was much too preoccupied by the parade of boyfriends that never seemed to end.

So if and when Meggie had visited the community pool, it was only to sit at the shallow end, dangling her feet, or maybe to wade in up to her waist. Ten cents seemed to be the magic number.

They even charged a dime to use the bathrooms, with little slot machines on the doors which wouldn't open without the deposit. Meggie remembered the one time she had actually begged a passerby for the funds to use the toilet, being a number two emergency situation. She had been quite amused by the graffiti written on the inside of the door:

Here I sit, broken-hearted, paid a dime, and only farted.

But the swimming lessons were never an option, so here she was … standing helplessly at the shoreline.

Kimmy continued to swim, jump, splash, and stand on her hands under water with her spindly white legs and feet splayed at the surface. She was laughing with utter delight as Meggie jealously and longingly looked on.

After awhile, Kimmy got bored with enjoying the water by herself, and exclaimed, "Let's take the boat out!"

Meggie was reluctant, because of both the frigidity of the lake, and her fear of what could be lurking out there in the deep, indigo water.

"Don't be a silly-willy! We can just sit in the boat and use our feet to paddle around! It will be *FUN*!" Kimmy could be quite persuasive in a demanding sort of way.

So Kimmy and Meggie arranged themselves in the little boat, which was just big enough for them to sit, back-to-back, with their legs dangling into the water from each end.

They floated around in the shallow end, where Meggie could still see the rocks and pebbles. This made her feel safe. But then Kimmy began to kick her feet and propel them to where they coasted above the mysterious darker water. Meggie clung to the soft plastic sides of the boat and leaned into Kimmy's back. The warm sun felt good on her goose-bumped skin, especially in contrast with the temperature-induced numbness in her calves.

Just as they passed the outermost end of the sun-bleached dock, Kimmy suddenly and *very* unexpectedly pushed herself out of the little blow-up boat with an exaggerated *SPLASH.*

Although Meggie was pretty scrawny, her weight on the one side instantly tipped the plastic vessel and quickly dumped her into the deep water. Before she went under, the icy coldness of it forced her to gasp in a deep, shocked breath.

She did not even make an *attempt* to swim. Meggie simply descended to the bottom, cheeks puffed out like a blowfish of some kind. Down … down … down she went, and as she was sinking, she gazed up at the surface of the water above her submerged body.

The sunlight glimmering off the small, undulating waves was like some beautiful optical illusion of light, and Meggie was mesmerized.

Her skinny little bum hit some slick, hard rocks at the bottom, and Meggie could no longer hold her breath. At first, the bubbles escaped through her nose as she attempted to retain oxygen, but her diaphragm, needing to expel the built-up carbon dioxide, forced the air out of her in a rush. That very same diaphragm then expanded involuntarily, meaning to pull in a fresh dose of air, but instead, the icy water was what was sucked into little Meggie's lungs.The sharp and intense pain of it lasted a millisecond.

That was all. Just a millisecond.

And then Meggie was strangely and suddenly filled with a sense of calm that she had never experienced in her young life. She felt like she was in the arms of the most loving, protective and strong mother … or father … or *some*thing.

Meggie was physically and emotionally *comfortable* in a way that defied description. She simply ... *felt.* And it was ... *good.*

Meggie looked again toward the surface, and watched as the lights that had been dancing on the waves above seemed to converge and cast a beam of very warm, soft light which was directed right toward her. She basked in this soft warmth, and the feeling that no harm would come to her—*ever*.

The cold, bony arms that abruptly encircled her waist were an unwelcome interruption. Meggie suddenly felt herself being pulled *up—up—up* in jerky movements. The next thing she knew, she was heaved out of the water and onto the splintery wood of the warm dock.

She began to cough and retch almost violently as her lungs desperately fought for oxygen.

As the wracking began to subside, Meggie became aware of the young girl at her side.

She could make out that the girl was a teenager, maybe fifteen or sixteen years old. She was extraordinarily pale, with freckles spattered over her face and shoulders. Her short, curly, and *very* red hair threw off a shower of the lake water as she shook her head and wiped at her eyes. "Are you okay?" she asked a bewildered Meggie, who had begun to cry, curling herself into a ball on the hard surface.

In the distance, Meggie could hear the piercing sound of Kimmy's screams, and then the confused exclamations of Kimmy's grandmother and Ms. Toni as they responded to the ruckus.

Meggie blinked the water from her eyes, then half-raised her head to respond to her rescuer, but when she looked back up, the girl was gone. Simply *gone*.

Instead, the anxious faces of Kimmy's grandmother and Ms. Toni filled the space and blocked out the sun, as one of them frantically shook Meggie's shoulders, shouting in a high-pitched shriek,

"MEGGIE! MEGGIE!"

When they came to the realization that Meggie was indeed alive and breathing, Kimmy's grandmother took the waif-like girl into her arms and began to weep. "You scared us, little Meggie," she croaked through her tears.

When Meggie groggily asked about where the red-haired girl had disappeared to, both Kimmy's grandmother and Ms. Toni stiffened, and looked at each with disbelief mixed with no small amount of shock.

"Are you sure it was a girl with curly red hair?" squawked her grandmother, while Ms. Toni simultaneously exclaimed,

"It *couldn't* be!"

After bundling Meggie in blankets, giving her a cup of hot cocoa and settling her and Kimmy onto the couch to watch *Mr. Rogers' Neighborhood*, the two women's almost fierce whispering could be heard coming from the kitchen. They could barely contain their excited chatter. It was mixed with that kind of awed tone when a particularly juicy piece of gossip is being shared, but there was also a tinge of dismay … almost *fear* … to their tone.

Meggie had always wondered what the women had been discussing, but it wasn't until years later when Meggie finally heard the story that would give her the shivers.

She hadn't seen nor heard from Kimmy since they were children, but from out of the blue, she got a phone call that would shed light and give her a basis for her belief that the red-haired girl had indeed been …

A guardian angel.

She met Kimmy at the cabin, which had not changed a bit since the last time she had been there. The one thing that had changed was Ms. Toni. She sat in a wheelchair, a home health nurse at her beck and call. Her body was failing her, yet her mind still sharp as a tack.

And she had a story to tell. It went like this:

The cabin on China Lake had belonged to Toni's family for generations. Her great Uncle Joe had spent entire summers there with his family.

His wife was a spit and fire Irish woman by the name of Sinead, and they had a daughter whom they called Shelley. Both Sinead and Shelley shared the genetic traits of their Irish blood, with pale, freckled skin and short, curly red hair.

One hot and muggy July weekend, Joe's brother, Jack, and his family came to spend the weekend at the cabin. Jack had a young daughter, Isabelle, who was only four years old. Shelly, at the age of 16 was old enough to babysit, so the adults had left her in charge of little Isabelle, while they drank wine and listened to music inside the cabin.

Although it was a hot day, the water remained quite cold. Shelley decided to let Isabelle play in their little rowboat that was tethered to the dock, as she lounged in the sun, trying in vain to get a semblance of a tan on her very alabaster skin.

She lay on a towel spread out on the wooden dock, only an arm's length from the boat.

But then Shelley fell asleep.

The rowboat somehow loosened from its mooring, and the craft quickly began drifting to the center of the lake.

Shelley jolted awake with a quick start just in time to see Isabella tumble over the edge of the tiny boat, which had coasted a good fifty yards away. She jumped into action, diving off the edge of the dock and swimming as hard and fast as she could. As she neared the area where Isabelle had sunk, she dove again and again, frantically and blindly, searching for the little girl.

She finally felt a small head, and pulled the child toward her by the hair until she could wrap her arms around her body, then pulled her to the surface.

As she came up from the depths of the dark blue water, Shelley's head hit the side of the rowboat with a rather loud crack.

She somehow managed to shove her tiny cousin over the edge and into the safety of the boat before losing consciousness and submerging to her own demise.

Jack happened to glance out the window to see what was happening. He sprinted to the edge of the water, where he dove in, swimming desperately to save his daughter. His first order of business was to administer resuscitation to the limp form of his most precious child. By this time, Joe had joined him and was repeating the very same dive and search that only minutes before Shelley had been doing to save Isabella.

Isabella survived, but it was hours before they recovered the body of Shelly, the beautiful 16 year old red-haired girl …

About the Author

Anne Katheryn Hawley was born and raised in the state of Maine. In addition to writing stories she is a portrait artist, fiddles around with the fiddle, and works part time as a Registered Nurse. She is married to singer/songwriter, Jim Hawley (pictured with Anne above, dressed as Titanic casualties for Halloween 2014) She has two children, Jessica and Jimmy, and one grandchild, Evan. She currently lives among the tall pines and crystal clear lakes of beautiful Northern Michigan.

Keep on the lookout for
Anne Katheryn Hawley's
next psychological thriller!

Killing Mom

Here's an excerpt:

Her heart pounded wildly in her chest. She could feel its rapid thumping in her ears. Her mouth was dry as a bone, yet her skin was broken out in a dripping, cold sweat.

Good … she thought, *at least my physical reaction proves that I have a conscience.*

The thought comforted her as she pushed 10cc of insulin, rather than the usual 10 units into her mother's abdomen. The difference between life … and death.

Her dear mother gazed vacantly at nothing.

Now it's just a matter of time … Claire thought as she shakily dropped the syringe into the Sharp's container at Mom's bedside.

Claire then knelt down to pray for forgiveness for breaking at least *two* of God's commandments.

Other novels by
Anne Katheryn Hawley:

Careful What You Wish For

Drowning was not exactly what Meggie had planned on, but ironically, it was drowning that saved her life … and her marriage … and possibly her soul. This is a twisting tale of fate, with a woven thread of other-worldliness. Things are not always what they seem. Expect the unexpected, and be *careful what you wish for*!

Worth More Dead

Anne Katheryn Hawley's debut novel is a psychological thriller about an average dysfunctional family, where the rivalry and jealousy between three sisters is raw and palpable.
Poor judgment, impulsive decisions, and very bad behavior result in a horrific tragedy – for which everyone pays a dear price.